Teddy Ruxpin's Bi

This story shows that fri...
are important every day of the year.

Story by:
Ken Forsse

Illustrated by:
David High
Russell Hicks
Rennie Rau
Theresa Mazurek
Allyn Conley/Gorniak

WORLDS OF WONDER™

Grubby™ Newton Gimmick™ Princess Aruzia™ Leota™ Wooly What's-It™

Prince Arin™ Fobs™

"Let's Sail Away Today"

Well, here we are in Mizley Meadows.

What are you doin' here in Mizley Meadows, Wooly?

Hey, here come the Fobs.
Hi, fellas.

Come on, Grubby, hit it!

Hi, Leota. That was a great flying catch.

Where's the cake and ice cream?